My Lantern and the Fairy

This book is edited and designed by the Editorial Committee of *Cultural China* series.

Story and Illustrations: Lin Xin
Translation: Yijin Wert

Copy Editor: Susan Luu Xiang
Editor: Wu Yuezhou
Editorial Director: Zhang Yicong

Senior Consultants: Sun Yong, Wu Ying, Yang Xinci
Managing Director and Publisher: Wang Youbu

ISBN: 978-1-60220-458-4

Address any comments about *My Lantern and the Fairy* to:

Better Link Press
99 Park Ave
New York, NY 10016
USA

or

Shanghai Press and Publishing Development Co., Ltd.
F 7 Donghu Road, Shanghai, China (200031)
Email: comments_betterlinkpress@hotmail.com

Printed in China by Shenzhen Donnelley Printing Co., Ltd.

1   3   5   7   9   10   8   6   4   2

My Lantern and the Fairy

A Story of Light and Kindness

Told in English and Chinese

By Lin Xin

Translated by Yijin Wert

Better Link Press

Long ago in the lamp stand on the village square, there lived a Little
Lamp Fairy. The villagers held a lantern contest every year to thank the
Lamp Fairy for bringing light and warmth to them.

传说村里广场上的灯台里有一位小灯神，为了感谢小灯神给全村带来光明
和温暖，村里每年都会举办花灯大赛。

One day, the eldest man in the village called everyone to the square. "The lantern contest is coming soon!" he said, "Everyone must present their most beautiful lanterns to participate in the contest."

这天，村里的长老召集大家来到广场。"花灯大赛就要到啦！"他说道，"大家要做出最美的花灯，比一比哦！"

The villagers got very excited. Some said that they would make dragon lanterns, and others said that they would make rabbit lanterns.

大家议论纷纷，有的说要做龙灯，有的说要做兔子灯。

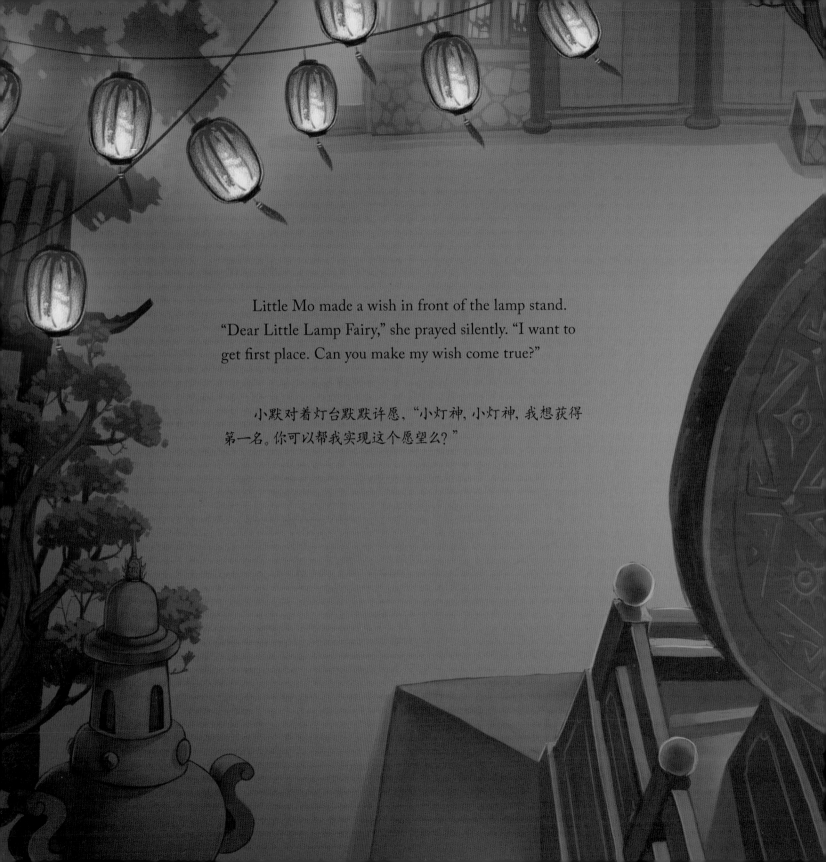

Little Mo made a wish in front of the lamp stand. "Dear Little Lamp Fairy," she prayed silently. "I want to get first place. Can you make my wish come true?"

小默对着灯台默默许愿，"小灯神，小灯神，我想获得第一名。你可以帮我实现这个愿望么？"

Boom! A sudden flash of lightening streaked across the sky. Then it started to rain!

"What if the flame in the lamp stand goes out?" Little Mo quickly opened her umbrella over the lamp stand to keep it out of the rain.

轰隆隆! 一道闪电划破天空。下雨啦!

"灯台里的火焰要是灭了该怎么办?"小默连忙打开随身带着的雨伞, 罩在灯台上挡雨。

As Little Mo was running back home in the rain, a big red flame shot up from the lamp stand and went straight after her ...

小默冒雨往家跑。一团红光随即从灯台升起，直追她而去……

After Little Mo ran into her house, she saw the red flame land on her shoulders. Her hair and clothes became dry instantly!

小默跑进家门，但见一团红光落到自己肩头，瞬间，她的头发和衣服就都干透了！

Little Mo was very surprised. "Who are you?" she asked.

"I am the Little Lamp Fairy. Thank you for keeping me dry with your umbrella. I am here to help make your dream come true."

小默惊讶不已，便问道，"你是谁?"

"我就是小灯神啊，谢谢你用雨伞为我挡雨，我是来帮你实现愿望的。"

"The Little Lamp Fairy is alive!"
The whole family was so happy that they
started to make a lantern together.

"原来小灯神显灵了呢！"全家人好开
心，便一起动手做花灯。

"The lantern should have a beautiful design," the Little Lamp Fairy said. When he heard this, Little Mo's father, a skilled craftsman, made a frame for the lantern. Little Mo helped him complete it.

小灯神说，"花灯要有漂亮的造型。"于是，会木活的爸爸制作了一个花灯的骨架，小默帮着爸爸一起搭。

1. Draw the design.

画出设计图。

2. Cut the bamboo culms into small segments and then split them into strips.

将竹子截成段，再劈成竹条。

3. Soften a bamboo strip with the heat of a flame, and then bend it into a desired curvature.

用火烤竹条，弯成想要的弧度。

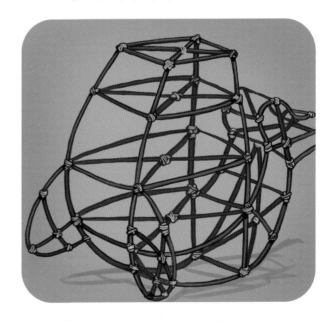

4. Follow the design to finish the frame of the lantern by tying the bamboo strips together.

将竹条绑成设计图上的样子。

"The lantern should have beautiful laces," the Little Lamp Fairy said. When she heard this, Little Mo's mother, a painter, drew the laces on the lantern. Little Mo helped her color the laces.

小灯神说，"花灯要有美丽的花边。"于是，会画画的妈妈为灯笼描上了花边。小默帮着妈妈填上颜色。

1. Paste the paper on the bamboo frame.

在骨架上粘上纸。

2. Gently draft the laces on the paper.

在纸上轻轻画上花边的轮廓。

3. Prepare ink and pigment.

备好墨汁和颜料。

4. Trace the outline of the laces with ink and fill them with colors.

勾轮廓，填颜色。

"The lantern should have interesting patterns," the Little Lamp Fairy said. When she heard this, Little Mo's grandma, an embroiderer, started to stitch decorative designs on the fabric. Little Mo helped her get the thread through the eye of the needle.

小灯神说，"花灯上要有有趣的图案。"于是，会刺绣的奶奶绣上了图案。小默帮着奶奶穿针引线。

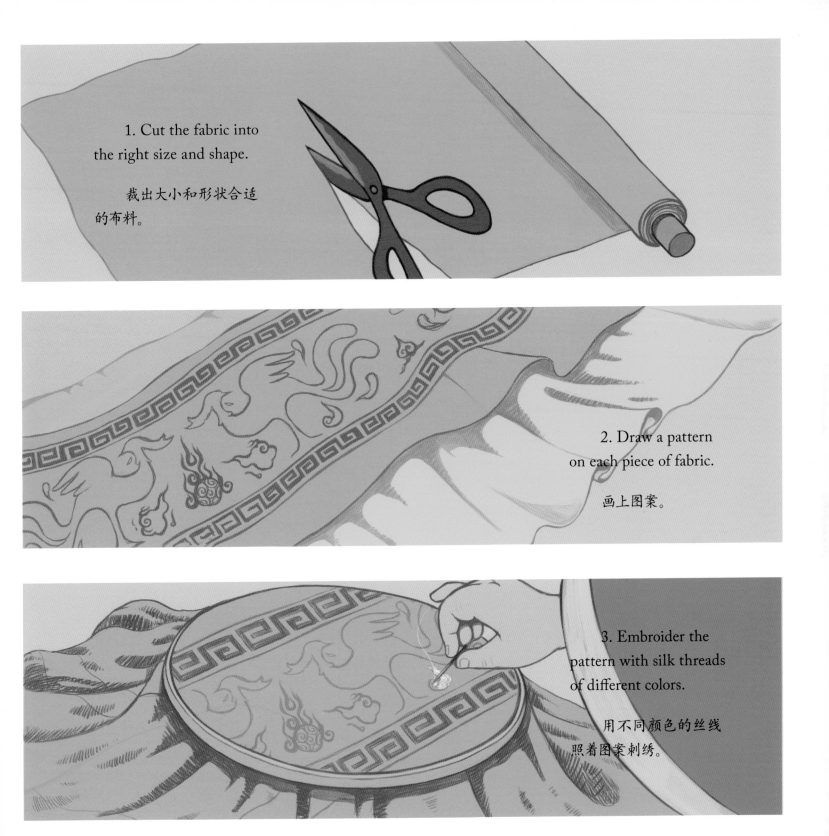

1. Cut the fabric into the right size and shape.

裁出大小和形状合适的布料。

2. Draw a pattern on each piece of fabric.

画上图案。

3. Embroider the pattern with silk threads of different colors.

用不同颜色的丝线照着图案刺绣。

"The lantern should have beautiful wood carvings," the Little Lamp Fairy said. When he heard this, Little Mo's grandpa, a wood carving artist, started to hand-carve many three-dimensional patterns. Little Mo handed the tools to him while he was carving.

小灯神说，"花灯上还要有精美的木雕。"于是，会雕刻的爷爷又雕上了许多立体的花纹。小默给爷爷递工具。

1. Find the right size pieces of wood.

找到大小合适的木头。

2. Draw a pattern on each piece of wood.

在木头上画图案。

3. Carve along the pattern.

沿着图案雕刻。

4. Paint the wood carving with colors.

给木雕上颜色。

Their lantern was finally finished! "Thank you for helping us design such a beautiful lantern," Little Mo said.

"I want to tell you that the rain actually cannot put out the flame in the lamp stand. You are so kind that I am sure your dream will come true!" The Little Lamp Fairy winked at Little Mo as she said this.

花灯终于完成了！"谢谢你帮我们设计了这么漂亮的花灯。"小默说道。

"其实雨水是浇不灭灯台火焰的。你那么善良，一定可以梦想成真！"小灯神眨眨眼。

The day of the lantern contest finally arrived. The square was full of people and all kinds of lanterns.

花灯大赛这一天终于到了，广场上好不热闹，到处都是各种各样的花灯。

However, Little Mo could not light her lantern. The lamp oil in the lantern had spilled on the way to the square because the roads were very bumpy. Little Mo was so worried that she was almost in tears.

可小默点花灯时怎么也点不亮，原来一路颠簸，花灯里的灯油都撒光了。小默急得都快哭了。

Just at that moment, the Little Lamp Fairy waved her magic lamp in her hand, and Little Mo's lantern suddenly became extraordinarily bright.

就在这时，小灯神将手中的神灯一挥，小默的花灯瞬间大放异彩。

Little Mo's lantern won first place as she wished. She jumped up and down with joy. "My dream has come true!"

小默的花灯果然夺得了第一名。她高兴得跳了起来，"我的愿望实现啦！"

As the Little Lamp Fairy winked at Little Mo, people saw a big red flame flying into the air, and then the whole village shined with dazzling brilliance.

小灯神向小默眨眨眼，只见一团红光飞到半空，整个村子被照得光彩夺目。

Cultural Explanation
知识点

Chinese lantern is a traditional folk craft. It is also a light source. In ancient times, people would surround a candle with a bamboo or wood frame and stretch silk or paper over it. People believe lanterns can expel evil influences and invoke blessings. It symbolizes the hope for a bright future. On holidays, people make a variety of lanterns.

花灯是中国的一种传统民间工艺品, 也是一种照明工具。在古代, 它用绢或者纸作为外皮, 用竹或木条制作骨架, 中间放上蜡烛点亮。人们相信花灯有驱魔求福的作用, 象征着对光明未来的向往。每到节日, 大家都会制作各种各样的花灯。

Chinese Lantern Festival: Enjoy lanterns, solve riddles on lanterns, eat rice balls to celebrate the coming of the new year.

元宵节: 赏花灯, 猜灯谜, 吃元宵, 共同庆祝进入新的一年。

Chinese Mid-Autumn Festival: Enjoy the Moon, eat moon cakes, light lanterns and wait for the family reunion.

中秋节: 赏月, 吃月饼, 点花灯, 企盼家人团圆。